RECORDARI

"Each of Blasko's collections have been personal, but this one holds the world in it. It opens a door into so many perspectives, yet ties them all together through a singular writer. It's one of the best collections I've ever read."
-Nathaniel Luscombe, editor of *Among Other Worlds*

"SJ Blasko mixes crushing vulnerability with empathy and introspection. She feels deeply for strangers, whether they are the "child on the floor of the library" or "the boy in the flower crown". I saw the world through her eyes; its longing, uncertainty and how we hope to grow beyond the sums of our regrets and fears. Her lines will stay with me and I highly recommend each line and sentence of this work."
-Ben Ditmars, author of *Type 2*

"SJ Blasko writes careful--and care-full--poems that speak to so many poignant and beautiful and funny and difficult moments of the human condition. This time, for me, "the boy with the flower crown" was the one I needed to greet inside myself, too. I see him. And he is happy."
-Robbie Walker, author of O Beautiful Dust: And Other Prayers While Walking in the Wilderness

Also by SJ Blasko:

Poetry:
Midnight Comes
the flowers need love to grow too
TREE

Short Fiction:
Losing the Stars

Featured Anthologies:
Space Kitties: Feline Forays Through the Galaxies
There is Us: a COVID-19 Anthology
Faces to the Sun: a Mental Health Anthology
Among Other Worlds
The Depths We'll Go To
Reconstructing Christmas

-

Recordari

25 poems for a hundred intimate strangers
by sj blasko

Recordari: 25 poems for a hundred intimate strangers
ISBN: 978-1-951882-06-8

Cover & formatting by SJ Blasko
Cover based on an image by Joshua Woroniecki
(joshuaworoniecki.com)

Dedication:

for every stranger in this book
<3

For the strangers I am proud of:

For the girl in her bedroom dancing to a silent music:

didn't your mother tell you not to leave
the curtains open and the
lights on
after dark?
didn't she tell you people will look in?
or do you know, and
is that why you dance as if for audiences
on your
hardwood stage and
sockfoot pointe?
(is there music? or is it only
you?)

For the boy I always see in dreams, vaulting over stairwells, running, running, running; chased and hunted and pursued; always one step ahead:

I hope that someday
you can run for love
and not in fear of it.

For the girl lugging her suitcase, backpack, & travel bag up and down the stairs at JFK/Umass:

Up and down, up and down
Lost and feverish and dizzy
You're pretty sure you missed your train
Your eyes are closing on their own
(how long have you been going?
how long have you been all alone?)
As you crumple,
Third trip up and down and up again those stairs
Dial that familiar number on your phone
(you've had it memorized since you were three and it
means home and home and home)
As you beg for help and swear you did your best
(darling, don't you know it's also holy
to let go and let your body rest)

For the girl who sits with her family in the same pew every week, pilot g2 moving furiously over pages of lines:

I see you, furrow in your brow;
wormwood in your mouth
are you picking? Tugging and
stretching and pulling?
Are you making sure that it is sound?
(are you finding out that it is not?)
You may lose the sweater, love
but that's okay
It was tight around the armpits
hugged your chest
and didn't hold your fidgety hands
And maybe in unwinding, in examining;
in handwashed baths in gentle soap
more dirt than you expected
will float up to the surface
Maybe you'll despair;
worry that you'll never end.
But when the washing and the weaving-back is done
you'll find that all the nettles
mystery thorns that pricked your skin
but you could never find
have been flushed out.
Maybe once you start rebuilding
you decide that sweaters aren't for you
(*maybe* all
those worms of string agree that *they*
are not so keen on going back to that)

But you have always loved cloaks
and scarves and hats that kiss the tips of your ears
in the frosty season
(y e s the tangles squiggle in delight)
And so, you make
                    together
And on the way, perhaps you are surprised
at strangers who will offer little
scraps of yarn from their own stores
Leftovers that fill in all the gaps and
light the work ablaze with colors you had never
dreamed before

Maybe you will never finish
blocking, sewing, patching up
picking out the leaves that come from
flying
climbing to the tops of trees and sobbing in the thinner
        air;
the way the world goes on below
while you are all alone up here.

Maybe you will never finish
never put it on without a phantom tingle or
stray thread
to block your way

Maybe you will never finish
That's okay, love,
that's okay.

To the child on the floor of the library, reading books they are supposed to be returning:

Darling, I see you
and my heart resonates like chimes in the breeze
You are thirsting
drinking knowledge from the pages
of fiction and stories
(the forbidden ones are not the sweetest
but they fill you up in ways that
other books have never done
even if the seeds stick in your teeth like raspberries)
You lap and wheedle; beg to
fill your bag and try to slip another
past your parents' watchful eyes
(you want to know *everything,*
even if the knowledge brings you to your knees).

To the girl in the green chair, who just introduced her boyfriend to extended family for the first time:

your aunt leans over
underneath the current of the room
"He's nice!" she says,
conspiratorially
"But if **you** break up with **him**,
I guess that we'll still love you"
a joke, but darling the relief goes
shooting through your veins unrivaled
by anything but cancelled plans &
isn't that far off.
(I think you thought
you'd gone too deep to save
like six years old and ocean swims
your feet had lifted from the ground and you had
>   *p   a   n   i   c   k   e   d)*

six months in he'd started dropping hints
(he was a distance runner, but
on circle tracks, you can't ignore much litter
before coming back around and end up falling)
(not the kind in love)
maybe you had hoped he'd stop
without your intervention
but- the way that ends is marriage
and if you do not want that
it doesn't matter if he does

you tucked that talk away for later
(you were not great at keeping secrets, though)

To the girl I only see in dreams:

You go back, and back, and back
returning to a place that hurts you
every time you enter through its doors

I don't know why
(i think i have a sense of it)

You want to still believe in good,
that people, flawed and all, can change
and hoping is not shameful, but

If they change, or when they do
(it is not cruel to make them to come to you)

To the girl in the west bridgewater library:

The librarians behind the desk
said they liked your hair, a mess of rainbow ends
You blushed, said thank you very much
but when just one
asked if you'd done it for Pride
your face lit up
You beamed, you almost cried
"Yes," you said, "i did; i did myself"
checked out your dvd and left
Your grandfather was waiting in the car
took in your blooming face and said
"Well you look happy."
You were not out;
throat swollen with forbidden things
the juice still stinging on your tongue:
"they liked my hair"

To the girl in union station, watching good omens for the first time:

You've got yourself all wedged
into a corner booth
phone propped up and headphones in
The stream is loading, loading, loading
on the shitty station wifi
You turn it off and try your data—it's no better
so you flip between the two like cable
buffer, buffer, buffer
as you trawl a starbucks fruit cup
hoping no one yells at you
(you don't know why they would, but it
seems always best to be prepared)
darting furtive glances towards
every stranger passing by
You relax a little past the intro
as if this is the first thing you've consumed
that has a God not painted as a man
has not painted adam white as snow
and eve as villain, criminal and executioner
(maybe it is, maybe eve is not

> buffer, buffer

pause to stab a watermelon chunk
the only person tasting of forbidden fruit today)

To the girl who came in for a wisdom tooth consultation; the doctor took one look and said, 'so we can take them friday, right?':

Sometimes
things just cannot be put off.

To the boy in the flower crown, holding his lover's hand as they walk down tremont street:

Oh.
You look happy.

To the stranger in the front of the bus, wrapped up in conversation with a man who shares your ex's name:

You tell this story as a joke:
the man who'd not stop talking,
the guy who kept you up when all you'd planned to do
was sleep
but i have seen
Inside the pages of your notebook
you wrote poetry about connection
stranger's stories, highway lights, and how
the world spins 'round and 'round
and yet we don't get vertigo
You kept his business card, my dear
and though the sands of time have ghosted
it away
Although you changed your phone and never put his
number in
Although you never talked again and
would not know him if you saw him now
You liked it.
Liked connection without consequential binding-to
Liked that for a couple hours
your two stories overlapped
on a crowded bus
bore witness to each other
existences both validated by a creature other than
yourself.

For the strangers I am proud of

(but in white)

To the boy who sits alone in the back of the bus and always stands before his stop:

It is
a practiced movement; let the driver know you're here
She's been driving you for years but lately you've been
skipping
and when you sit you slouch
Anyway, you slug your backpack on one shoulder
(the chiropractor says that's bad; the chiropractor has
been seeing you
since you were six; you're far too tired for both straps
so he will have to deal and patch you back together)
The last seat on the bus might be
your favorite part of school
Maybe you picked it up from watching upperclassmen
You're the senior now; you don't like violence but
you'll punch an upstart freshman who thinks that he
can take your spot
(you won't. maybe you're a chicken, maybe he is, maybe
you've both joined the pecking order)
Sometimes they try to fvck with you; poke the bear
you put your headphones in and *glare*
rest your head against the window's edge and feel its
every rattle, clank and bump. Your house is almost last
You stand just past the one before; sling your backpack-
But, we've covered that—and let the rocking motion
Carry you.

For the girl who never thought she was desirable:

In sixth grade a boy came up to you
surrounded by his friends.
"do you want to go out?"
he asks and just to clarify you ask
"out where?"
"like out" he says
(you don't want
to presume)
It was a dare
you turn him down
"thank God" he says
that doesn't hurt you

(it's okay, though
if it hurt you just a little bit)

For the girl standing in the ocean, arms floating like jellyfish limbs atop the waves:

It is not silly
to do things that make you happy
to do things for you, with no one watching
or even to perform for subtler audiences
the strangers you can
always sense around
(the ocean is not empty—there are
swimmers, surfers; fish)
The problem lies when you forget
to stop performing
(you are all the witness
that your joy and pleasure need)

**For the girl with undiagnosed anxiety who goes to the
nurse with a stomachache every time the class is
assigned a writing prompt:**

Two boys
taught you how to crack your knuckles
on a bench outside the main office
The nurse had gotten a call, and, well
she couldn't leave you trouble-sorts alone
So you came with, three short-legged beasts
tromping just behind
and while she was inside, you found that you could be
distracted
from your stomach, (which had felt
like it was flipping 'round and 'round
opening a little wider every time
to swallow you up whole)
by the new sensation of popping knuckles
in and out of place
like machinery
Of keeping up with the boys, this once,
until the nurse came out
and saw that you were smiling and declared
you couldn't be that sick if this was all it took
to cheer you up
And sent you back to class

She didn't believe your protests
and I think this was the first
(but not the last time)

that the truth was not believed as it was
falling from your lips

and in your gut the panic flared anew

For the boy in the brockton waiting room:

Your heart rate spikes
And you duck behind your hood, your hair, your phone
Hoping that the months since you have seen her last
Will hide the details of your face
People always say that you look younger
than you are
Like time has deemed your face
a canvas not worth painting on—and
usually that's fine
But not right now, your heart rate spiking
as your first therapist walks through the room
looking for her client
(*not you, not you, not you*)
She's the fourth adult who's ever made you angry
but all you feel right now is
fear and fear and fear
that
she will see you, know you; you will have
a panic attack within these walls
(you don't know how to name those yet
much less how to share them and moreover
you don't want to
she'd barely gained your trust the first time
when she broke it and
you'd rather drown than let her have it now)

To the pair of black boots in the bathroom, hiding sick and shuddery breaths between the stalls:

Don't worry, no one hears you
(don't worry, love, I do)
Don't worry, you are not the only one
to feel like this and hide
(don't worry, I still do it too)

For the tenant on floor two who came down so many times to check the mail in one day that the landlady laughed at them and said "i'll ring your doorbell when it comes":

Good things come to those who wait
But sometimes good things wait to come
to those who really need them, too.

To the girl who walked into the new hampshire applebees and tried to pick up a pizza:

I bet you never thought you'd have to ask "what store is this?"
post-walking-in deliberately
You looked lost, confused,
endearingly, I think
You looked the kind of person who's been long and well-acquainted (painfully) with phone-call-stress
and restaurant bathrooms
accepting mixed up orders instead of asking for another
"I ordered on the phone?" you say
hand curled around a fidget toy
They look at you like you're a little crazy
(does applebapple even offer that?)
You give your name, they say
"there's nothing here?"
I see it crash across your face "what store is this?
I don't think that this is right-"
You booked it out—halfway across the mall
you found where you were supposed to be

it's okay to be a lot bit lost.

To the girl who entered genki ya in boston, out of breath, got halfway through "gyoza" no less than four times, and tripped on "sal-mon sal-ad" too:

"did you run all the way here?"
the waiter asks, but they are smiling so
you blush and shake your head
"take a breath" he says, and so you do
"gyoza and a salmon salad?"
"tobiko but no mayo, please"
"about ten minutes" so
you sit down at the counter

try to slow your racing heart

text your lover *"i would publicly
become a fool for you <3"*

To the girl sitting on rocks in hanover:

I see you shuffling your shoulders
to point your fandom sweatshirt
towards the road
Toss your head and let your hair
                              fall
like the heroine
you scribble in your book, or read
(i don't remember; that's okay)
i think that you are beautiful.
and i don't think it's silly
to be out looking for your *own*.

For the girl in the store, spending money she does not have on things that bring her temporary joy:

Today I am not of a mind
to be compassionate

(that does not mean you don't deserve it)

To the stranger in the bodega, whose card declined on a $15 box of gloves:

I'm sorry, love
I wish that I had more to give
but these hands of mine were made for loving
not for working to the bone
And I have yet to find a workplace that
will break the bank
(instead of breaking me.)

To the one sitting on the stairs at church, eyes closed, hands curled around a little bear:

You are healing, healing, healing
(healing is not linear)
You are going, going, going,
(remember how we said
it's holy too to rest?)
You are growing, growing, growing
(sometimes even giants have
to shrink back down
to fit inside a cellar in a storm)
You are breathing, breathing, breathing
(slow down, my love. the air will not
desert you here)
You are healing, healing, healing
(you can only do your best).

Dedication, ii

*For every stranger in this book
and the **me** we all became*

After-words, or
For you: the only other person in this book:

The boy on the bus wants you to know
that they're okay now
No longer looping, drowning, riding
that same bus to that same place
every day
(he has broken the cycle)

The girl between the shelves
wants to say that she's forgiven herself
for deception
for lies,
(even if the only one still hurting
is herself)

The child thirsting after knowledge
is still hungry
But we've finally stopped
rationing ourself
(it turns out, when you are not drinking poisoned water
you can consume so very much more)

the author wants you to know
that there were only ever two people in this book
you
and her
(this collection could never have been anything but
autobiographical)

Acknowledgements

My lover lies asleep on my lap, and I promised I'd be done in 10 more pages (9 pages ago) so I will keep this brief.

Thank you to everyone in my life, present and past, who I loved. You helped me make myself.
Thank you to my love. You inspire me to keep making myself <3
(Also thank you to my mom & dad—I guess y'all made me first)

This book wouldn't have been possible without my lovely beta readers: Nathaniel, Ben, Calliope, Lief, Ziel, and especially Mariella.

And lastly, this whole book was inspired by Morgan Harper Nichols's own collection: Storyteller. If you liked this, go read that.

Thank you, too, reader.
I hope you're happy with who you've become.
That's all.

About the Author

SJ Blasko (she/they/he) is a Bostonian poet and jack of all trades. As a disabled LGBTQ+ Christian, much of their work revolves around the intersections of mental health, chronic illness, queerness, faith, and identity.

You can keep up with their frequent book yelling and (semifrequent) posts on instagram: @thesongsofsparrow.